October

When it's <u>WINDY</u> DON'T FORGET!

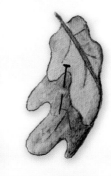

Monday	Tuesday	Wednesday	Thursday	Friday	Saturday	Sunday	NOTES
		1 MUSHROOM HOPPING WITH NIM ?	2 See KAY about ACORNS	3	4 HAZELNUT FESTIVAL	5	Remind Nim about LeaF-Catching RECORD attempt THIS MONTH
6	7	8	9	10	11	12 LAST PICNIC OF THE YEAR (bring WOOLLENS)	
13	14 Get seeds with Edie for bird friends	15	16	17	18	19	
20	21	22	23	24	25 Dormice's hibernation supper R.S.V.P. ← done	26	
27	29	28	30	31 Nov 1 GeT polecat Mae WiTH PiNCH PUNCH (fiRST of MONTH)			

The Hubble & Hattie imprint was launched in 2009, and is named in memory of two very special Westie sisters owned by Veloce's proprietors. Since the first book, many more have been added, all with the same objective: to be of real benefit to the species they cover; at the same time promoting compassion, understanding and respect between all animals (including human ones!)

In 2017, the first Hubble & Hattie Kids! book – *Worzel says hello! Will you be my friend?* – was published, and is joined by *The Lucky, Lucky Leaf*, the first book in the Horace & Nim series, as well as the books pictured below.

Other books from our Hubble & Hattie Kids! imprint

9781787111608

9781787113077

9781787112926

www.hubbleandhattie.com

First published September 2018 by Veloce Publishing Limited, Veloce House, Parkway Farm Business Park, Middle Farm Way, Poundbury, Dorchester, Dorset, DT1 3AR, England. Tel 01305 260068/Fax 01305 250479/email info@hubbleandhattie.com/web www.hubbleandhattie. com ISBN: 978-1-787113-06-0 UPC: 6-36847-01306-6 © Chantal Bourgonje, David Hoskins & Veloce Publishing Ltd 2018. All rights reserved. With the exception of quoting brief passages for the purpose of review, no part of this publication may be recorded, reproduced or transmitted by any means, including photocopying, without the written permission of Veloce Publishing Ltd. Throughout this book logos, model names and designations, etc, have been used for the purposes of identification, illustration and decoration. Such names are the property of the trademark holder as this is not an official publication. Readers with ideas for books about animals, or animal-related topics, are invited to write to the publisher of Veloce Publishing at the above address. British Library Cataloguing in Publication Data – A catalogue record for this book is available from the British Library. Typesetting, design and page make-up all by Veloce Publishing Ltd on Apple Mac. Printed in India by Parksons Graphics.

The Lucky, Lucky Leaf

Horace & Nim

Chantal Bourgonje and David Hoskins

With special thanks to Su Dore and Cathy Hookey

It was a wild and
windy autumn day
in the forest.

Nim, Horace
and Edie were
marching along
happily, kicking
up the leaves
and singing.

It looked like they were having fun, so Kay joined them.

"Where are we going?" asked Kay.

"We're off to where the tall trees grow to catch falling leaves."

"If you catch a falling leaf, it's lucky," said Horace.

"Why is catching falling leaves lucky?" asked Kay.

"It's a superstition," said Horace.

"Isn't a superstition just another way of saying it's made-up?" asked Kay.

"Better a superstition than a normalstition," said Nim.

Nim often said things that Kay didn't quite understand.

7

They soon arrived at the place where the tall trees grew.

Edie and Horace did their warm-up
exercises, while Nim closed his eyes
and stood quite
still.

"What's Nim
doing?" asked
Kay.

"He's going to try to break his record of catching five lucky leaves before teatime," said Horace. "He's getting into the zone."

"It's not easy catching leaves," said Edie.

"I'm hopeless at it," said Horace. "But I like it."

And with that they started.

And it was true.
They were hopeless.

They didn't catch a single leaf.

Kay couldn't catch a single leaf either.
But it was fun trying.

"I don't know what's
wrong with these
leaves," said Kay.
"They're not normal.
They've got minds
of their own!"

"That's very true," said Nim. "You've got to out-think them."

Nim was ready to start.

Horace and Edie sat down to watch, and Kay joined them to see how Nim did it.

He was amazing.

Sometimes he chased a leaf ...

... and other times he waited for the leaf to come to him, his hands darting out at the last minute.

He caught one leaf

Two

Three leaves.

Four.

And five! Five lucky leaves.
Nim had equalled his record!

"Hurrah," they all cried.

But then something
happened.

17

Nim couldn't seem to catch another leaf.

Not a single one.

"Maybe he's trying too hard,"
said Horace.

"It's the pressure,"
said Edie.

Nim tripped and landed in a puddle.

Edie helped him up.

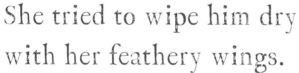

She tried to wipe him dry
with her feathery wings.

Then he ran through a patch of
angry old stinging nettles and
stung himself.

Horace applied the cream.

And then Nim tried extra, extra, EXTRA hard ...

... but he lost his balance and landed head first in a bramble patch.

He had prickles everywhere.

Even on his bottom.

Kay felt the giggles coming on as they all helped
pluck out the prickles.

And then Nim smiled too.

"Look!" he cried. "I managed to hold on to it. That's six. I've broken my record. I'm the luckiest hare in the forest!"

"To be honest," said Kay, "you don't look like the luckiest hare in the forest. You look like a bit of a soggy mess."

Nim looked at his scratches.

And his wet, muddy fur.

He felt his stings stinging away.

And his smile disappeared.

"I see what you mean," he said. "I wonder what went wrong?"

"Of course," said Kay, "you're lucky enough to have friends who are there to wipe you dry when you landed in a puddle."

"Friends who put cream on your legs when you got stung," said Edie.

"And pluck the prickles from your bottom when you landed in the brambles by mistake. That's pretty lucky," said Horace.

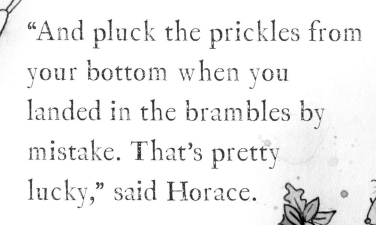

"That's very lucky," said Nim.

And as he said it,
another leaf landed
on Nim's nose.

"A seventh leaf!" said
Horace.

"And seven is a lucky
number!" cried Nim.
"That's a lucky,
lucky leaf. I really
am the luckiest
hare in the
forest."

28

He jumped for joy.

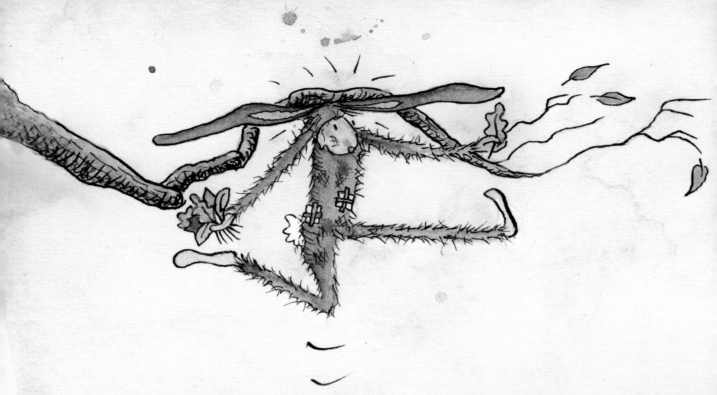

And hit his head on a low-hanging branch.

"Oh Nim!" they all cried.

"Perhaps that's enough good luck for one day," said Nim.

Everyone agreed.

And with a new personal best for Nim, they all went happily home for tea.